11.95

Jackie French

Jackie French's writing career spans 12 years, 36 wombats, 102 books for kids and adults, nine languages, various awards, radio shows, newspaper and magazine columns, theories of pest and weed ecology and 28 shredded back doormats. The doormats are the victims of the wombats, who require constant appeasement in the form of carrots, rolled oats and wombat nuts, which is one of the reasons for her prolific output: it pays the carrot bills. Her most recent awards include the 2000 Children's Book Council Book of the Year Award for Younger Readers for *Hitler's Daughter*, which also won the 2002 UK Wow! Award for the most inspiring children's book of the year; the 2002 Aurealis Award for Younger Readers for *Café on Callisto*; and ACT Book of the Year for *In the Blood*.

For more on Jackie French, her wombats and her books, zap onto her website: www.jackiefrench.com or subscribe to her free monthly newsletter about her books and wombats at: www.harpercollins.com.au/jackiefrench

Stephen Michael King

Stephen's first picture book, *The Man Who Loved Boxes*, was nominated for the Crighton award for illustration, was the winner of the inaugural Family Award and was selected for Pick of the List (US). He has since illustrated over 20 books, and has been shortlisted five times for the Children's Book Council Awards. In 2002 he won both the Yabba and Koala children's choice awards for *Pocket Dogs*.

Stephen and his family live on a coastal island in a mud brick house on 10 acres of organic orchards, rainforests and visiting wildlife.

P9-DNK-650

Books in the series:

My Dog the Dinosaur
My Mum the Pirate

Watch out for these upcoming
Wacky stories in 2004:

My Dad the Dragon
My Uncle Gus the Garden Gnome

OXFORD COUNTY LIBRARY

My Mum the PIRATE

Jackie French

illustrated by

Stephen Michael King

Angus&Robertson
An imprint of HarperCollins*Publishers*

Angus&Robertson
An imprint of HarperCollins*Publishers*, Australia

First published in Australia in 2003
by HarperCollins*Publishers* Pty Limited
ABN 36 009 913 517
A member of the HarperCollins*Publishers* (Australia) Pty Limited Group
www. harpercollins.com.au

Copyright © Jackie French 2003
Illustrations copyright © Stephen Michael King 2003

The right of Jackie French and Stephen Michael King to be identified as the
moral rights author and illustrator of this work has been asserted by them
in accordance with the *Copyright Amendment (Moral Rights) Act 2000* (Cth).

This book is copyright.
Apart from any fair dealing for the purposes of private study, research,
criticism or review, as permitted under the Copyright Act, no part may
be reproduced by any process without written permission.
Inquiries should be addressed to the publishers.

HarperCollins*Publishers*
25 Ryde Road, Pymble, Sydney, NSW 2073, Australia
31 View Road, Glenfield, Auckland 10, New Zealand
77–85 Fulham Palace Road, London W6 8JB, United Kingdom
Hazelton Lanes, 55 Avenue Road, Suite 2900, Toronto, Ontario M5R 3L2
and 1995 Markham Road, Scarborough, Ontario M1B 5M8, Canada
10 East 53rd Street, New York NY 10022, USA

National Library of Australia Cataloguing-in-Publication data:

French, Jackie.
  My mum the pirate.

  ISBN 0 207 19949 3

  1. Family – Juvenile fiction. 2. Pirates – Juvenile fiction.
  I. King, Stephen Michael. II. Title (Series: French, Jackie,
  Wacky families).

A823.3

Cover and internal illustrations and design by Stephen Michael King
Typeset in Berkeley Book
Printed and bound in Australia by Griffin Press Pty Ltd on 80gsm Econoprint

7 6 5 4 3 2 1   03 04 05 06

To everyone at North Rocks Primary ...
I promised you a dedication and here it is!
PS: It's a pretty fantastic school, too.
JF

For Taden, Siobhan, Ellie, Kaitlan,
Shauna, and their piratical parents.
SMK

CHAPTER 1

A Pirate Crew

'I'll slice your gizzard!' yelled Mum, waving her sword at the fleeing slaver captain. 'I'll chop your toes off to feed the fishes!'

The battle raged across the decks of the pirate ship *Mermaid*. Swords clashed, seagulls yelled. Down on the lower deck, the pirates had caught half the slaver crew in the net Filthy Frederick used to catch sea monsters. Up on the mast the skull and crossbones fluttered in the breeze.

Mum leapt down the stairs, grabbed the slaver captain by his greasy pigtail and gave him a kick in the backside with her long black boot, sending him over the rails and into the water.

'Take that, snot whiskers!' she yelled. She peered into the coil of rope where Cecil was sitting with his books. 'Have you finished your homework?'

'Not yet,' said Cecil. 'It's hard to concentrate with all the noise going on. It's this really hard maths problem ...'

'I don't care if it's advanced alchemy; I want that homework done before bedtime ... Take that, you undercooked son of a seasick gorilla!'

'But Mum,' shouted Cecil, as Mum leapt up back onto the bridge after another slaver, 'what's the cube root of twenty-seven?'

'Three!'

Filthy Frederick's wooden leg clattered across the deck. 'Sorry, me hearty,' he yelled to Cecil. 'But your mum's busy at the moment!'

Another slaver leapt down from the bridge and onto the coil of rope.

Swack! Filthy Frederick's wooden leg kicked him overboard.

'Say hello to the sharks, you pile of seagull vomit!' yelled Filthy Frederick, picking a cockroach out of his beard and absent-mindedly eating it.

'Are there any sharks down there?' asked Cecil, interested.

'Of course not,' said Filthy Frederick.

Cecil quickly took a final breath of clean air as Filthy Frederick sat on the edge of his coil of rope. Filthy Frederick was one of Cecil's favourite people in the universe, but sometimes Cecil wished he'd take a bath.

'Oof! Time for a breather, me hearty,' said Filthy Frederick, grinning and showing his three long, yellow teeth. 'I'm not as young as I used to be. No, your mum would be cross if anyone got hurt in one of her battles. You know what she says: "Free the slaves, grab the treasure and don't get any bloodstains on my clean deck." Any more maths problems?'

Filthy Frederick had once been thrown in a dungeon with the king's mathematician who'd been silly enough to argue when the king said two times four was nine. Filthy Frederick had learnt lots of things in that dungeon, like the cube root of lots of numbers (including seven hundred and twenty-nine) and never argue with someone who has a crown and an army.

'A pirate's life is the way for me,' sang Filthy Frederick, swinging his wooden leg around and knocking another two slavers into the ocean.

'With lots of enemies on the sea,

With chests of treasure and jewels too,

A fine free life for me and you! '

'See you later, me hearty,' added Filthy Frederick to Cecil. 'Best get back to the battle!' He heaved himself

up, leaving a small cloud of
fleas behind. His wooden leg
tapped on the deck after
another slaver.

'See you later, Filthy
Frederick,' said Cecil.

'Snap!' agreed Snap,
peering out of the coil of rope.

Snap was Cecil's pet crocodile. Mum reckoned no
one was going to try to grab Cecil if he had a crocodile
on guard.

'Glop.' Snap swallowed what looked like a couple of
fingers and grinned at Cecil.

Cecil grinned back. Mum said Snap wasn't allowed
to eat fingers or toes or even a nice chunk of slaver's
bum, but Cecil reckoned that sailors on any ship that
carried slaves deserved whatever they got.

Cecil turned back to his homework. Behind him the
fight was nearly over. Filthy Frederick and Mum were
pushing the last of the slavers off the plank.

Ambrose One Arm and Harry the Hook were
carrying half the treasure chests from the slaver ship to
theirs.

Barnacle Bruce was explaining to the bewildered
slaves on the deck of the other ship that the ship was
theirs now and so was the other half of the treasure, so
they were rich. And, by the way, did anyone know how

to sail a ship because if not, he'd give them sailing lessons.

Down in the sea the slavers were swimming over to the small desert island nearby. Mum made sure there was an island nearby when she made prisoners walk the plank or tossed them overboard, and if one of them couldn't swim, she threw him a lifebelt.

'Jelly-bellied sons of a sea serpent slavers!' snorted Mum, striding back over to Cecil and wiping her sword on her trousers before sheathing it in its scabbard. 'I hope the crabs crawl up their underpants and bite their ...' She remembered Cecil was listening. 'Well, son, how's the homework going?'

'Nearly done.'

'Good. Dinner'll be ready in three shakes of a dolphin's tail. Hey, Putrid Percival!' she shouted. 'What's for dinner?'

'Sea monster stew!' came the answer from down in the galley.

'But we had sea monster for lunch and breakfast and last night's dinner!' yelled Mum.

'Can I help it if all you blighters catch me is sea monster?'

'How many maggots in the ship's biscuit then?'

'One thousand, four hundred and twenty-two!' called back Putrid Percival.

'Not enough,' decided Mum. 'You need at least five

thousand maggots in a barrel of ship's biscuit to make it tender enough to get your teeth into. Let's have pizza. That all right with you Perce?' she called.

'Fine by me,' Putrid Percival called back. 'I've been boiling the tentacles for three hours, but they're still too tough to chew.'

'You lads,' bellowed Mum to the pirate crew. 'You want sea monster or pizza for dinner tonight?'

'Pizza!' yelled Filthy Frederick, aiming his armpit at a slaver who was trying to climb back on board. The slaver fell back into the sea as the smell overpowered him.

'Pizza!' cried Barnacle Bruce.

'Pizza!' shouted Harry the Hook.

'Without any anchovies,' called Shark-eyed Pete. 'Those maggot munchers put anchovies on my pizza last time. You know they make me burp!'

'Snap,' agreed Snap, breathing rotten fish and chewed up fingers all over the deck. Snap liked pizza even better than toes and fingers.

'Make mine lasagne!' announced Ambrose One Arm.

'Right, eight pizzas and one lasagne, and make sure they don't put any sea monster on my pizza. Make sail for shore, lads!'

Mum threw Cecil a bag of gold. 'Take these down to the rare coin shop when we get to Bandicoot Creek and order up the pizzas, will you? Get some of that white stuff too. What's it called again?'

'Milk,' said Cecil.

'Right,' agreed Mum. 'Nine tankards of their best milk too.'

Cecil sighed as he shoved his homework back into his bag.

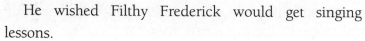

He wished Mum and the crew had never discovered pizza.

He wished Filthy Frederick would get singing lessons.

He wished Snap could learn to use a toothbrush.

But most of all, he wished he didn't have to go to school tomorrow.

CHAPTER 2

Cecil's Birthday Wish

It wasn't that Cecil didn't like school. He *did* like school. He liked playing football with the other kids at lunchtime. He loved learning lessons and reading books. In fact, that was how the whole problem began.

It had been his birthday. The whole ship had a holiday every year on Cecil's birthday.

'Even if the *Black Ship* sails by,' swore Mum, 'it's not going to interrupt the party!'

'But we'd have to chase the *Black Ship*!' protested Cecil. The *Black Ship* was the biggest, worst, slave ship on the whole Spanish Main. Mum and the crew had tried to catch it many times, but the *Black Ship* was too big and too fast.

Mum shrugged. 'We'd never catch it anyway,' she muttered. But then she grinned. 'Let's forget about the *Black Ship*, me hearties!' she cried, waving her sword in the air. 'Let's have the best birthday party ever!'

Cecil woke early on his birthday. His hammock rocked gently between the poles in his bedroom. Through the porthole, he could see the sun sparkling on the sea.

Cecil pulled on his stockings and pantaloons and shirt and pirate hat, and headed out into the passageway.

Someone had decorated the companionway with pirate flags, and long ropes of skulls (Filthy Frederick carved them out of driftwood) hung all around the galley.

'Happy birthday, matey,' called Putrid Percival, stirring a pot of sea monster soup on the stove.

'Happy birthday, lad!' yelled Harry the Hook, and Filthy Frederick and Ambrose One Arm and Barnacle Bruce.

'Happy birthday!' yelled Shark-eyed Pete, putting the last touches to Cecil's giant birthday cake. It was shaped like a pirate ship and the candles poked out of tiny cannon. There were even some chocolate slavers walking the plank into a sea of blueberry jelly.

Snap grinned at Cecil from under the table and said 'Snap', in a happy-birthdayish sort of way.

'Happy birthday, son!' cried Mum, putting her tankard of tea down on the table and kissing Cecil on the cheek.

'Happy birthday to you!

Happy birthday to you!

Happy birthday, dear Cecil,

From all of the crew,' sang Filthy Frederick, absent-mindedly squashing a cockroach as it ran out of his shirt and up his neck.

The presents spilled all over the table. Cecil sat down and opened them.

There was a pirate ship in a bottle from Harry the Hook and a giant skull with a candle in it that Filthy Frederick had carved for him, a spoon carved out of a shark's jaw from Shark-eyed Pete and a new shirt with the skull and crossbones on it from Ambrose One Arm. Barnacle Bruce had knitted him a bright red hat with

three pom poms, and Putrid Percival had made him a big box of toffee-coated sea monster.

One last present sat on the floor. It was an old sea chest. Mum grinned. 'Aren't you going to open it?' she demanded.

Cecil nodded. He lifted the lid. Snap slithered over and peered in too, just in case there was a nice dead body to eat.

There wasn't a body. Or diamonds. Or jewels . . .

'Books!' cried Cecil. 'A whole chest of books!'

Mum grinned. 'We captured it two ships ago,' she explained. 'We hid them in the hold till your birthday. Those books were going to the King of Spain,' she added. 'But you'll make better use of them. Now, I suppose you're wondering what I've got you?'

Cecil nodded.

'Well, I was thinking, what would a lad your age want? A new sword? But you don't like sword fighting. A cannon of your very own? But you can use the ship's cannon whenever you want. And then I thought: I want my son to have whatever *he* wants!'

'So,' said Mum, taking a big gulp of tea, 'what would you like? A chest of treasure? A crown with rubies and diamonds? A shrunken head to hang in your bedroom? A small island? A pet leopard? Anything, lad! It's yours!'

Cecil bit his lip. There was just one thing he wanted, one thing he wanted more than anything else. He gulped.

'What I'd really like,' he began.

'Yes?' said Mum.

'More than anything else . . .' said Cecil.

'Anything!' said Mum.

'I want to go to school,' said Cecil.

Chapter 3

You Want What!

'School!' yelled Mum. Her tankard of tea dropped from her hand and hit Snap on the head, though as he was a crocodile with a crocodile's hard head, he didn't notice.

'Yes,' said Cecil.

'A son of mine going to *school*?'

'Yes,' said Cecil.

'But no one in our family has ever gone to school!' protested Mum.

'I never went to school,' Mum continued. 'Your dad never went to school. We've always been pirates! Grandpa was a pirate, Grandma was a pirate, your Aunt Mary has her own ship over in the gulf! Great Granddad was a pirate, Great Grandma was . . .'

'But I don't want to be a pirate,' said Cecil quietly.

'Not a pirate!' cried Mum. The crew looked shocked. 'Why not?' yelled Mum.

Cecil tried to work out how to explain.

'I get seasick,' he said.

'Not since we gave you that turtle dung and vampire bat potion,' objected Mum. 'You didn't even vomit up the sea monster custard Putrid Percival made last week!'

'I don't like sword fighting either,' explained Cecil.

'Then get your crew to do the fighting!'

'I don't like navigating by the stars. I ... I ...'

Suddenly Mum stopped yelling. 'What do you like?' she asked softly.

'I like books!' cried Cecil desperately. 'I like reading and writing and things like that. And the only way to get a job reading and writing is to go to school.'

Harry the Hook scratched his head with his hook. (Harry the Hook had two good hands, but he reckoned that if two hands were useful, then two hands and a hook were even better.)

'Lad's right,' he said to Mum. 'You can't make the lad into a pirate if he doesn't want to be one.'

'He's a reader all right,' offered Filthy Frederick. He picked a piece of sea monster out of his long, grey beard and chewed it thoughtfully. 'Some kids are weird that way,' he added.

'The problem is,' said Ambrose One Arm, 'how can a pirate kid go to school?'

Mum scratched Snap's horny back with her boot. Snap grinned happily, showing all his crocodile teeth. He loved having his back scratched.

Then Mum nodded. 'So be it!' she declared. 'Cecil goes to school. But not just any school! No being sent off to study with the monks or sitting with a pimply tutor for Cecil! I want my son to go to the best school in the world! Listen well, you landlubbers!'

'Yes, Captain,' they chorused.

'We need to find ourselves a wizard!'

Chapter 4

The Wizard

The pirate crew had to capture three more slaver ships before they found a wizard.

The battle on the slaver ship raged around as the wizard stepped up on deck. He wasn't much of a wizard. His robe looked like Mum's second-best dressing gown and had gravy stains all down it, and someone had sat on his pointed hat, so now it was a squished and squashed hat instead. But he still had an air about him that wasn't *all* last night's fish dinner, as he trod onto the deck and looked about him.

'Hold!' he cried, as the swords clashed about him. 'I am a wizard . . .'

'Are you now?' muttered Filthy Frederick, shoving his trousers down and aiming his bum at a fleeing slaver. 'But you can't magic iron, and swords are made of iron, so get out of the way before someone cuts you!'

'But I ...' The wizard stopped as the fleeing slaver turned green, then purple, then collapsed from lack of breatheable air.

Filthy Frederick hauled his pants up again and turned back to the wizard. 'Captain will see you as soon as she's got a spare second! So scoot! Climb over the rails onto our ship, where you'll be out of the way!' ordered Filthy Frederick.

The wizard blinked. Then he clambered over to the good ship *Mermaid*, avoiding the grappling hooks that held the two ships together. He looked around then sat on a pile of rope and watched as Mum leapt up the companionway and poked the slaver captain in the bum with her sword. The captain jumped and turned around, just as Mum cut his belt so his pants fell down and ...

'Hi,' said Cecil.

The wizard blinked as Cecil climbed out of the pile of rope and sat next to him. 'What were you doing in there?' demanded the wizard.

'Keeping out of the way,' said Cecil frankly. 'Mum says I get underfoot when there's a battle on. This is Snap.'

'Snap,' said Snap.

The wizard eyed Snap warily. 'What's a crocodile doing on board ship?'

'He's a pet. Didn't you ever have a pet?'

'I had a toad once,' volunteered the wizard. 'He ate the flies in the kitchen.'

'Snap eats things too,' explained Cecil. 'Leftover sea monster or chopped-off toes and stuff lying round after the battles. Filthy Frederick said we could just throw the rubbish overboard, but Mum said, "No, that's polluting."'

'Snap!' said Snap. He chewed something thoughtfully.

'What's he eating now?' inquired the wizard.

'Best not to ask,' said Cecil.

'Oh, right,' agreed the wizard. 'Your mum's the pirate captain?'

Cecil shook his head. 'She's a privateer really,' he corrected. 'Good Queen Bess gave her permission to capture Spanish slave ships, as long as we share the treasure with her. And with the slaves too, of course.'

The wizard nodded. 'I see,' he said. He watched the battle with interest.

Ten minutes later, the slavers had walked the plank and Mum was cleaning the blood from her sword. (She hadn't stabbed anyone. The blood was from the roast sea monster they'd had for lunch. But Mum said a nice bloody sword was a great way to frighten evil captains.)

'Bunch of hairy-bummed baboons,' she muttered. 'Those slavers are lower than a whale's belly! Avast there, matey!' she yelled to Shark-eyed Pete. 'Get the slaves up on deck and explain they're free, will you? I need a tankard of tea.'

She caught sight of the wizard. 'Who would this poor cockroach be?'

'He's a wizard,' explained Cecil, sliding off the pile of rope. 'He was being kept prisoner on the slaver ship.'

Mum eyed the wizard doubtfully. 'If he's a wizard, how did they keep him prisoner?'

'It was the iron,' said the wizard. 'Magic can't touch iron. As long as they had me chained, I was helpless. They were planning to sell me as a slave.'

'Bunch of two-toothed toe-jam chewers,' snorted Mum. She looked the wizard up and down disbelievingly. 'Well, mayhap you're a wizard and mayhap you aren't. But whoever you are, you're free now.' She began to stomp down to the galley.

'Hold a while,' said the wizard quietly. 'I want to thank thee.'

'No thanks needed,' said Mum. 'Just keep thy guard up when slavers are nearby.'

'Please,' said the wizard. 'Wizards always pay their debts.'

Mum sighed. 'So be it. Let's say you are a wizard. Then there's only one thing I want.'

'A bigger ship?'

Mum snorted. 'The *Mermaid*'s the best ship that ever sailed the seven seas!'

'A better crew?'

'There's no better crew on any boat afloat,' said Mum loyally.

She hesitated. 'No, there's something I want for my son. My son is more precious to me than any treasure in the world. He's a fine son. But he likes reading. I've got naught against that, of course — some of my best friends can read, and they're none the worse for it.'

'True,' said the wizard. 'I've known some fine people who could read, and not all of them in dungeons.'

'Well, you see,' said Mum, 'being a reader and all, the lad wants to go to school. And if that's what he wants, I want him to have it. I want him to go to the best school in the world.'

The wizard looked at Cecil, then he looked at Mum. Then he nodded. 'Sail towards the sun for seven days,' he said. 'Then turn left at the next star. You'll sail through a time warp and your son can go to the best school in the world.'

Mum blinked. 'What's a time warp . . . ?' she began.

It was too late. A cloud of silver stars shimmered on the deck. The wizard had disappeared.

Mum blinked. 'Shiver me timbers! That poor cockroach really was a wizard!' she exclaimed.

Ten days later, Cecil was at Bandicoot Flats Central School.

And three months later, it was almost Parent–Teacher night, and Cecil was wishing he'd never ever heard of school at all.

Chapter 5

The Problem With School

Cecil looked out the classroom window. There was the tuck shop with the oval below it, and beyond that was Bandicoot Creek, flowing sluggishly down to the ocean. Down in Bandicoot Cove, Mum, Filthy Frederick and the rest of the crew waited on the good ship *Mermaid* for him to come home from school, so they could sail back through the time warp and hunt for a slaver ship or two before dinner.

It was hard just to sit in a classroom all day, after being able to roam around the ship as it sailed the seas. But school was interesting too, and that made up for it. Cecil had learnt a lot in the months he'd been at school.

He'd learnt that long black boots and a pirate hat weren't correct school uniform.

He'd learnt to talk like everyone else.

He'd learnt that even if your teacher gave you too

much homework, you couldn't make them walk the plank.

He'd learnt that carrying a cutlass, or even a musket or blunderbuss, got you sent to the principal's office.

He'd learnt what TV was, and Game Boy, and how to order takeaway pizza.

He'd learnt about prime numbers and whole centuries of history that hadn't even happened yet on board the good ship *Mermaid*.

He'd learnt that calling himself CJ instead of Cecil was a *really* good idea.

He'd learnt that kids at school gave heck to anyone who was a bit different.

And he'd learnt that the worst thing in the world would be if *anyone* found out that his mum was a pirate.

'Right,' said Mr Farthingale, 'homework tonight is the problem on page thirty-six and the spelling list on

page fifty-three. And remember, it's Parent–Teacher night tomorrow! It starts at eight and there'll be tea and coffee in the library.'

The bell jangled just as he added, 'Class dismissed.'

Cecil shuddered. Parent–Teacher night! He could just imagine what would happen if Mum swaggered into the school hall in her boots and pirate hat and sword!

Thank goodness he'd thrown away the note so Mum hadn't seen it! He'd just have to make up some excuse: say she was too busy or had to go out tomorrow night.

There was no football practice that afternoon. Cecil sauntered out the door, over the netball courts and out the front gate.

'Hey, CJ,' yelled Shaun from the bus stop. 'Want to come over this arvo? Jason and I are renting a video.'

'I . . . er.' Cecil hesitated. It would be great to go over to someone's place, just like a normal kid. And he'd never even seen a video. He shook his head regretfully. 'Sorry, I can't. I told Mum I'd be straight home.'

'Give her a ring then.'

Cecil gulped. How did you explain that you lived on a pirate ship with no telephone? 'Er . . . the phone's out of order,' he said.

'My dad says most of the phones round here don't work half the time,' said Shaun cheerfully. 'See you tomorrow then!'

'Yeah. See you.'

Cecil walked slowly down the street. Even if Mum hadn't expected him back on the good ship *Mermaid*, there was no way he could have gone to Shaun's place. If you went to someone's place, then they'd expect to come to your place and ... and ...

Cecil shook his head sadly. How could you ask friends home to a pirate ship?

It was about a twenty-minute walk to the cove where the good ship *Mermaid* lay at anchor. Cecil walked up the street from the school and through the Bandicoot Flats shopping centre. He was just crossing the road by the pizza shop when a voice hailed him. 'Ahoy, young fellow-me-lad!'

Cecil turned. It was Filthy Frederick. He limped over to Cecil, seven pizza boxes in his hands.

'Your mum sent me out for pizza!' he explained, squashing a slug that had crawled down his trousers, with his wooden leg. 'I'll walk home with you.'

Cecil looked round quickly. But no one from school was watching, and anyway, Filthy Frederick had taken off his pirate hat to come into town. He'd even tied back his long, grey hair in a ponytail and combed the sea monster chunks out of his beard. A few passersby looked sympathetically at his wooden leg and one bare horny foot, or looked around to try to find where the smell was coming from, but most ignored them.

'How was school, lad?' asked Filthy Frederick, his wooden leg tapping as they walked along the footpath, and his fleas dancing on his collar in the sunshine.

'Okay,' said Cecil.

'Me and the crew would love to see that school of yours one day,' said Filthy Frederick wistfully. 'What were those things you said could talk to anyone right around the world?'

'Computers and the internet,' gulped Cecil. He

had a horrible vision of the entire pirate crew turning up at Parent–Teacher night or, even worse, at the school sports.

'Amazing,' said Filthy Frederick, shaking his head.

Cecil crossed his fingers. 'Parents and, er, friends aren't allowed to come to the school,' he said. 'It's a very strict rule.'

'Well, if it's a rule, we'd better obey it,' said Filthy Frederick. 'Don't want them lashing you to the mast and flogging you with a cat o' nine tails, do we lad? Or tar and feathering you, or shutting you up in the school dungeons, or . . .'

'Afternoon CJ!'

It was Mr Farthingale. Cecil tried to sink into the concrete, doggy doo and all. 'Good afternoon, sir,' he whispered.

29

Mr Farthingale smiled at Filthy Frederick. 'Is this your father?'

Filthy Frederick grinned over the pile of pizzas, showing his remaining three long, yellow teeth. 'Shiver me timbers! I'm not the lad's father! His dad died in the big typhoon when Cecil here was just a little snapper. No, I'm ...'

'My great uncle,' put in Cecil hastily. 'This is Great Uncle Frederick, Mr Farthingale. *Great Uncle* Frederick, this is Mr Farthingale, my teacher.'

'Pleased to meet you,' said Mr Farthingale. He sniffed. 'Someone must have left a bag of prawns in one of the rubbish bins,' he said.

'Teacher!' Filthy Frederick beamed. 'Shiver me timbers and caulk my bulkhead, I never thought I'd meet a real live teacher! I was just saying to the lad here, how much his ma and me and the boys would love to see that school of his.'

'Why not come to Parent–Teacher night then?' asked Mr Farthingale.

Filthy Frederick frowned. 'What's Parent–Teacher night?'

Mr Farthingale frowned. 'Didn't you give your mother the note about the Parent–Teacher night, CJ?'

'Er. Um,' said Cecil. 'She's really very busy. I don't think ...'

'So what is this Parent–Teacher night?' boomed Filthy Frederick over the pizza boxes.

'It's when parents and teachers can talk about how kids are going in class, and parents can see some of the work the class is doing,' explained Mr Farthingale. 'It's tomorrow night.'

'Shiver me timbers!' roared Filthy Frederick again. He gave Mr Farthingale such a smack on the back (while keeping a tight hold on the tower of pizza boxes) that he nearly fell into the gutter. 'The lad's ma will be there all right! The whole crew will be there!'

No! thought Cecil desperately. No! Maybe he could run away and join the circus! He could learn to juggle and teach Snap how to jump through hoops.

Maybe he could find another wizard to give him wings so he could fly away *fast* before Parent–Teacher night!

Maybe he could . . .

Filthy Frederick nodded at his pile of pizzas. 'Better get these back before they get cold or the captain'll have my guts to tie the sails with! Pleasure to meet you, M'lord Teacher.'

Cecil bit his lip as they walked away. Mum and the crew coming to Parent–Teacher night! What could he do now?

Chapter 6

Parent Teacher Night

The deck of the good ship *Mermaid* was scattered with pizza boxes and burnt crusts. The skull and crossbones flapped merrily in the breeze. In the shade of the mainsail, Snap chewed on crusts and Shark-eyed Pete's anchovies.

Mum took a last bite of her pizza supreme and wiped her hand over her mouth. 'That was the best dinner I've had since we captured the king of Spain's chef the day your dad and I got married,' she said happily. 'Now, I'd better get meself tidied up for this Parent–Teacher night. What do you think I should wear, son? My new black boots and the lace shirt with velvet jerkin?'

'Um,' said Cecil. 'Most of the other mums will be wearing dresses, or maybe tracksuit pants . . .'

Mum laughed so hard a pizza box nearly blew over the rail. 'A dress! I'd get my sword tangled in my petticoats!'

'But Mum, women don't wear great big skirts and petticoats any more. They don't wear swords either,' he added hopefully.

'No sword! What if we run into some slavers?'

'There aren't any slavers in Bandicoot Flats . . .' began Cecil.

'Or footpads or bandits? No, son, I'd feel undressed without my trusty sword at my side. That was the sword I wore when I married your dad, the sword I wore the day you were born . . .'

'Look, Mum, you don't *really* want to come to Parent–Teacher night! It'll be boring!'

'Fa de la!' cried Mum. 'I've never seen a school before! Or met a teacher! Filthy Frederick said your teacher was a fine figure of a man, too! Now, are any of you landlubbers coming to Parent–Teacher night with us?'

'Parent–Teacher night's just for parents,' put in Cecil quickly, then felt mean as Filthy Frederick's face fell.

'Snap?' asked Snap hopefully, crawling up to Cecil's feet and grinning with his giant, yellow teeth.

Cecil shook his head. He felt worse and worse. 'It's not for crocodiles either,' he added. Snap slunk sadly back to the shade of the mainsail.

'Never mind, lads,' said Mum comfortingly, 'I'll tell you all about it afterwards. Tell you what, why don't you lads pick us up afterwards?' she said to Filthy Frederick. 'Sail the dinghy up Bandicoot Creek. Bring the crocodile too. It'll be an outing for him. Save Cecil and me walking back in the dark.'

'But Mum, we can take a taxi.'

'A taxi! When there's a good dinghy going idle!' Mum shook her head. 'And this way the crew can get a look at the school too. Come on. We don't want to be late.'

CHAPTER 7

MUM GOES to School

The school hall was already crowded when Mum and Cecil arrived. The buzz of conversation stopped as Mum strode in, her best pirate hat set jauntily on her long black hair, her big leather boots shining in the light, the giant ruby on her finger flashing red.

'Who's that?' someone whispered.

'It's CJ's mum.' Someone snickered. 'She must be on her way to a fancy-dress party!'

Cecil led Mum quickly across the hall to Mr Farthingale's table. Mr Farthingale's eyes widened as they approached. He glanced down at Mum's sword, her ruby ring, and her lace-covered bosom, and gulped.

'Er, Mr Farthingale, this is my mum.'

'Pleased to meet you, Mrs . . .?'

Mum grinned. She thrust out her hand. The giant ruby flashed again in the hall lights. 'Tania the Terrible. Just call me Captain Tania.'

'Er ... Captain Tania.' Mr Farthingale looked stunned as he shook Mum's hand. 'Please sit down. Now CJ has really been doing very well.'

Mum beamed. 'That's my boy!' she exclaimed.

'A bit weak in his maths but he's improving steadily.'

'Don't fret yourself now,' said Mum, patting his hand so her ruby flashed even brighter. 'Filthy Frederick's been helping him. Frederick studied with the king's own alchemist, you know.'

Mr Farthingale blinked. 'The king ... alchemist? Oh. Good,' he said faintly. 'Well, I hope we'll see you at the football match this Saturday.'

Mum frowned. 'Football?'

'It's a game,' hissed Cecil. 'That's what I do on Saturday mornings.'

'Football?' Mum's forehead creased even more. 'You play it with one foot? You hop maybe? Or do the team all have wooden legs?'

'No, two feet. You kick the ball around.'

'Then it should be feetball!' declared Mum. 'I've never been to school but even I know it's two feet, not two foots. Can parents come to these feetball matches?'

'Of course. The more people who come the better,' said Mr Farthingale, who was now openly staring at Mum's ruby ring, sword and lace-covered bosom.

'Wonderful!' boomed Mum.

36

She clapped Cecil on the back. 'You young varmint! Why didn't you tell me parents could come to the feetball matches! The crew and I will be there, swords at the ready. In case there's a bit of trouble,' she added to Mr Farthingale. 'You never know when a trusty sword will come in handy!'

'Er, yes, I mean no,' stuttered Mr Farthingale. He stood up. 'Perhaps you'd like a cup of tea,' he suggested a bit weakly.

'Never say no to a tankard of tea,' smiled Mum. 'Best thing to come out of China since gunpowder and cannon. Good evening to you, teacher!'

'Er . . . Good evening to you too,' said Mr Farthingale. He looked even more stunned now.

Cecil quickly steered Mum over to the tea table. It was almost over now! 'Look, are you sure you want a cup of tea?'

'What's your hurry, lad? The dinghy isn't even here yet.' Mum picked up a styrofoam cup and looked at it critically. 'This the best they can do? Give me a good pewter goblet any day! Fill 'er up, son, and let's drink to your school days.'

'Er ... could you speak more quietly, Mum,' whispered Cecil, embarrassment crawling up from his stomach to his face as Mum hoisted her styrofoam cup against his. 'You're not on board ship now!' Tea cascaded onto the floor but Mum didn't seem to notice as she swigged hers down.

'What use is a captain if her men can't hear her?' boomed Mum. 'This is good tea, son! Fill 'er up again.' She held out her styrofoam cup.

'How about a biscuit?' asked Cecil desperately. 'Two biscuits ...' If Mum's mouth was full, she'd have to be quiet.

'Any maggots in the biscuits?' demanded Mum.

'No,' said Cecil.

'Then they'll be too tough to chew,' said Mum.

'No Mum, really, modern biscuits don't need an axe to break them,' began Cecil.

'Ah, CJ, I was looking for you.'

Cecil turned. It was Mr Pootle, the football coach. 'I'm afraid I've had to drop you from the team this Saturday,' said Mr Pootle. 'You weren't quite as fast as you could have been last week.'

Cecil tried not to sound disappointed. 'That's all right, sir.'

'*What* did you say?' Mum crashed her styrofoam cup down on the table. It split, sending the last of the tea splashing onto the plate of orange cream biscuits. 'You're dropping my son from the feetball team?'

'Um ...' Mr Pootle looked stunned. Most people looked stunned when they first met Mum, thought Cecil. 'Just temporarily, you understand.'

'My son *likes* the feetball team!' roared Mum.

'Mum, look, it's okay,' hissed Cecil.

'The crew and I were going to watch him next Saturday! The crew really *want* to see this lad play feetball!'

Mum reached for her sword

Oh, no, not the sword! thought Cecil. Please not the sword.

Mum raised the sword high into the air. 'Do you want to visit Davy Jones's locker, you jug of cockroach slime?' she yelled. 'Do you want me to feed your gizzards to the fishes?'

'Wha — what?' stammered Mr Pootle.

'I'll keelhaul you, you pile of dragon guts!' cried Mum. 'I'll make you walk the plank!'

'Look ...' trembled Mr Pootle, eyeing the sword as Mum waved it through the air. 'He can play next Saturday! I promise!'

'Giving in are you? You lily-livered, snot-nosed sea snake!' Mum prodded Mr Pootle in the stomach with her sword. She hated people who didn't stand up for what they believed in. 'Are you a man or a jellyfish?'

Everyone was staring at them now. People started crowding round.

'Please,' whimpered Mr Pootle. 'He's back in the team. Just put the sword down.'

Cecil closed his eyes. It can't get any worse than this, he thought. This is the most terrible moment of my life.

But he was wrong.

CHAPTER 8

The Crew Arrive

'With a yo ho ho and we'll raise the flag,
We've lots of cake in a paper bag.
We've six watermelons and pizza too.
It's a pirate's life for me and you!'

The sound of singing — well, something like singing, anyway — floated up from the creek. The splash of oars and a muttered 'Heave and ho, heave and ho' came faintly through the doors, under the sound of Filthy Frederick's song.

Mum slid her sword back into its sheath and clapped Mr Pootle on the back so hard he nearly fell into the milk jug. 'There's the crew come to pick us up. No hard feelings then?' she boomed. 'The lad is back in the feetball team and . . .'

'Football,' said Mr Pootle faintly.

Mum stared at him. 'What sort of snot-brained teacher are you? If you've a wooden leg then maybe it's football. But if you've two strong feet, then feetball it has to be!'

'Er, yes, quite right,' said Mr Pootle weakly. 'Feetball, that's it.'

'Good man!' declared Mum. 'Come on, Cecil! The crew awaits! Time and tide wait for no man or woman!'

She strode out of the hall just as Filthy Frederick and the boys started another verse:

'With a yo ho ho and a pirate ship,

A big cream bun and a nice egg flip.

A pirate's life is bold and free,

A grand fine life for you and me.'

'A grand fine life for you and me!' carolled Mum, waving her sword again so the jewels in its hilt cast red and green flashes on the hall walls. 'Coming Cecil?'

Cecil slunk out of the hall.

The giggles followed him.

CHAPTER 9

The Day After is Even Worse

It rained the next day. The grey waves lapped at the good ship *Mermaid* and the drops pounded on the deck above as Cecil pulled on his school uniform.

'Fried sea monster or muesli?' asked Putrid Percival, as Cecil trudged into the galley for breakfast. 'Or Harry the Hook caught a giant octopus yesterday. Could do you a nice dish of scrambled seagull eggs and octopus.'

'Just muesli please,' said Cecil.

'You sure? That muesli was fresh in yesterday. No time to get any weevils yet to add a bit of flavour.'

'I don't mind,' said Cecil. He spooned his muesli slowly, but it was no use. He just wasn't hungry. Cecil sighed and shoved his muesli under the table for Snap to finish. Snap didn't like muesli much, even if it had weevils in it, but Snap would eat anything for Cecil.

If only I didn't have to go to school today, thought Cecil desperately. If only I was like everyone else at school. If only my mum was anything except a pirate ...

'Good morrow, everyone,' muttered Mum, stomping into the galley in her boots and sword and dressing gown. Mum was never at her best before breakfast. 'A tankard of tea, please Putrid. A big one.'

She took a deep drink then smiled at Cecil. 'Good night last night, son,' she said. 'Good to get a goggle at where my son spends his days.'

'Mum,' said Cecil pleadingly, 'maybe ... maybe it's not such a good idea for me to go to school. I just don't fit in there! Maybe I really could be a pirate.'

Mum put down her cup of tea. 'Do you like sword play?' she inquired.

'No,' said Cecil. 'The swords are too big and sharp.'

'Do you like sailing into the sunrise with a fresh wind at your back?'

'You know I get seasick unless I take my potion — and it tastes like snot,' said Cecil.

'How about watching the stars above you at midnight, as you set your course for the Barbary Coast?'

'I get a crick in my neck looking up at the sky for too long,' said Cecil.

'What do you like then?' demanded Mum.

Cecil considered. 'Well, reading books, and computers, and football.'

'Feetball,' corrected Mum.

'Feetball,' said Cecil. 'And stuff like that.'

'Then you still don't want to be a pirate,' stated Mum.

'I suppose,' said Cecil unwillingly.

'So go to school,' said Mum, picking up her tankard of tea again. She glanced out of the window at the rain. 'Would you like a lift today? It's really wet out there. The boys could row the dinghy up the creek again.'

'No, really, thanks Mum,' said Cecil hurriedly. 'I like the walk up from the cove. It's good exercise.' How could he possibly explain to Mum, he thought, that no one else at school arrived by boat!

'Well, have a good day,' said Mum, kissing his cheek. 'Watch out for giant octopuses and tidal waves and typhoons.'

'There are no octopuses or typhoons at Bandicoot Flats,' said Cecil. 'But, yeah, I'll take care. Have a good day pirating.'

Mum shook her head. 'We'll just have a quiet day scrubbing out the forecastle. I'll make sure Putrid here has a nice drop of hot sea monster soup for you when you get back.'

'Thanks, Mum,' said Cecil glumly.

'Have fun,' said Putrid Percival kindly, as he splashed tomato sauce on the sea monster tentacle he was frying for Harry the Hook's breakfast.

Fun, thought Cecil gloomily. He grabbed his school bag and trod slowly up the companionway. Something slithered behind him. Cecil turned. There was Snap, laboriously crawling up the stairs, on his short crocodile legs, behind him.

'What are you doing, old boy?' asked Cecil.

'Snap,' said Snap. He rubbed his head against Cecil's leg, leaving a greasy mark made up of old fingers and stale tentacles and fresh muesli on Cecil's tracksuit daks.

'Have you come to comfort me?' asked Cecil.

'Snap,' agreed Snap.

Cecil sighed and scratched Snap's back with his

jogger. 'It's all right, old boy. I'll be fine. It can't be that bad at school.'

'Snap,' said Snap.

'All right,' said Cecil, 'it *will* be that bad. But I can cope. Really.'

Snap watched him sadly as Cecil tramped up the stairs and out onto the wet deck.

Chapter 10

A Terrible Morning at School

It was raining even harder as Cecil pulled his tiny dinghy up onto the sand and squelched up the beach. The sea was grey, the sky was grey and Cecil felt grey too.

Water poured down the gutters as he walked up the footpath, through the shopping centre, then down the hill again to school. Even school looked grey — its playing fields and oval all sodden and puddly, and the school buildings dull with rain.

Cecil walked through the school gates. He could feel

the stares as soon as he entered. Someone pointed at him and giggled. He heard the word 'pirate' as he turned the corner by the library.

Jason and Shaun came up to him as he put his bag among the others on the rack outside the classroom. Jason nudged Shaun, and Shaun nudged Jason.

Finally Jason said, 'We saw your mum at the hall last night.'

'Yes,' said Cecil shortly.

'Was she really going to attack Mr Pootle with her sword?' asked Shaun.

Cecil tried to laugh. 'No, of course not! It was just a joke.'

'Mr Pootle didn't look like he thought it was a joke,' said Shaun. 'He looked like he was going to wet his pants.'

'Well, it *was* a joke,' said Cecil, even more shortly. 'Mum was going to a fancy-dress party afterwards. It wasn't a *real* sword, of course.'

'It looked real,' said Jason.

Cecil gave a sickly grin. 'Of course it wasn't real! Whoever heard of a mum with a sword!'

Jason glanced at Shaun. 'I suppose,' he said, as though he wasn't really convinced.

'Look,' began Cecil desperately, just as the bell rang for morning assembly.

Cecil breathed a sigh of relief. Saved by the bell! For the first time he was actually glad to go to morning assembly!

Chapter 11

A Message From the Principal

The next hour wasn't too bad. Mr Farthingale kept giving him strange looks, but at least no one said anything about pirates or swords or attacking sports masters in the school hall.

In fact Cecil was hoping that maybe everyone would forget about Parent–Teacher night when one of the third-graders knocked on the door.

'Message from Mrs Parsnip,' she said. Mrs Parsnip was the school principal. 'Would CJ please go to her office immediately.'

Cecil gulped. Mr Farthingale looked at him a bit sympathetically as he stood up. 'Off you go, CJ,' he told him.

Cecil grabbed his raincoat and headed out into the mud. He had never realised it was such a long way to Mrs Parsnip's office. His feet seemed too heavy to ever get there as they trudged through the puddles.

There was a kid already sitting on the hard wooden seats outside Mrs Parsnip's office. He smirked at Cecil. 'What are you here for?' he asked.

Cecil recognised him. It was Big Bernie, the school bully.

'Don't know,' said Cecil.

Big Bernie smirked again. 'I have to sit here till the end of the period,' he said, then put on a silly voice, 'because I was "disrupting all the others".'

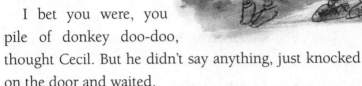

I bet you were, you pile of donkey doo-doo, thought Cecil. But he didn't say anything, just knocked on the door and waited.

'Come in.'

Mrs Parsnip looked up from her desk. ' Ah, CJ,' she said. 'I'm afraid I've had some complaints about the disturbance in the hall last night.'

'Oh. Sorry, Mrs Parsnip,' said Cecil meekly. 'Mum was just going to a fancy-dress party and got a bit carried away.'

Mrs Parsnip looked at him sternly. 'Waving a sword about and threatening to attack a teacher is more than just being carried away.'

'It was a joke!' protested Cecil.

'Well, I, for one, don't think it was funny. Neither did Mrs Bumpus, the president of our Parents and Citizens Committee. In fact Mrs Bumpus suggested,' Mrs Parsnip cleared her throat, 'Mrs Bumpus is afraid that your mother might believe she really is a pirate!'

'But . . .' began Cecil.

'It seems Mrs Bumpus met your mother down at the pizza parlour last week. She says your mother was wearing pirate clothes then too. Surely there wasn't another fancy-dress party?'

'Um,' said Cecil trying hard to think of something that would explain his mum.

'Now, CJ, of course it's not your fault if your mother is a little . . . peculiar.'

Cecil blinked. 'My mum isn't peculiar!'

'Well, really, wearing a pirate costume all the time and waving a sword about isn't exactly normal . . .' Mrs Parsnip began.

Suddenly Cecil lost his temper. Mum might be embarrassing, but she was also the bravest pirate on the whole Spanish Main! And she was his mum, and she'd always done her best for him and . . . 'Mrs Bumpus is a batty old barnacle!' hollered Cecil.

'CJ!' cried Mrs Parsnip.

'My mum's not crazy at all! She really *is* a pirate! She got this wizard to send me to the best school in the world, but if he thinks this is the best school, then he's a pretty dumb wizard!'

'You don't really think . . . Your mother can't *really* be a pirate, CJ!'

'Well, she is!' yelled Cecil. 'And she's a lot more interesting than boring Mrs Bumpus!'

'CJ, do you really *believe* your mother is a pirate?' shrieked Mrs Parsnip.

'Yes!' shouted Cecil, 'and she's a really good one.'

'Well,' huffed Mrs Parsnip, looking at him as though she thought he was crazy too. She frowned. 'I think perhaps I'd better ask your mother to come in and have a . . . a chat with me.' She glanced down at Cecil's file. 'I don't seem to have her phone number.'

'We don't have a phone,' said Cecil. Suddenly he felt light enough to float up to the ceiling. It felt *good* not having to pretend any more. 'You don't get phones on pirate ships!'

Mrs Parsnip looked bothered. 'Well, her work number then . . .'

'She's a pirate!' exclaimed Cecil. 'She goes to work on her pirate ship!'

'The sooner I have a chat with your mother the better,' muttered Mrs Parsnip under her breath. Then she said, more loudly, 'All right, CJ. You can go back to your class now. But I expect to see your mother tomorrow!'

Cecil slunk out of the office. How dare Mrs Parsnip criticise his mum!

Big Bernie smirked at him. 'That was *really* interesting! I heard every word!'

'Oh, go feed your fingers to the fishes,' muttered Cecil. He was too upset to worry about Big Bernie now. He tramped back through the rain to his classroom.

Chapter 12

All Over School

It was all round the school at lunchtime. Big Bernie must have told *everyone*, thought Cecil dismally.

But at the same time he felt sort of glad that the secret was out. Secrets were a heavy weight to carry and anyhow, so what if he was different? So what if Mum was different?

So what if Filthy Frederick had cockroaches in his beard and sounded like a seagull with laryngitis when he sang, or Harry the Hook had a hook as well as his two hands, or Ambrose One Arm had only one arm and two teeth, or Putrid Percival spent all day cooking sea monsters? They were his family!

The rain pelted down onto the asphalt. Cecil sat in a damp corner by himself and tried to chew his sea monster sandwiches and stared at the rain.

'Hey, CJ!'

It was Shaun and Jason. 'What do you want?' muttered Cecil grumpily.

'We just wanted to ask, is your mum really . . .?'

'Yes!' yelled Cecil. 'She really is a pirate! So go away!'

'You don't have to yell,' said Shaun.

Jason nudged him. 'Leave him alone for a bit,' he hissed. He hesitated, then said, 'We're over by the hall if you want to sit with us.'

Their footsteps splashed across the asphalt.

Cecil didn't even look up. He didn't want to sit with anyone. He didn't want to speak to anyone. He just wanted to eat his sandwiches and keep the tears from falling . . . Anyway, now he wasn't hungry.

Cecil threw his sandwiches in the bin and stomped off to the library, where he could be alone.

CHAPTER 13

Rain

It rained all through lunch. It rained all through maths.

Cecil looked at his watch. Only another hour to go and then he was never coming back to school, *ever*. He'd become a pirate even if he had to drink turtle dung and vampire bat seasick potion all his life, even if he got a stiff neck from watching the stars, even if it meant leaving behind the library and the computers and all the books ... And your friends, said a small voice in his brain.

'They're not my friends!' Cecil told himself. No one would want to be friends with a kid from a pirate ship!

He looked at his watch again. Fifty-eight minutes till the bell ... Suddenly the bell pealed, over and over. Cecil looked at his watch again. It must be slow! But the bell kept on ringing and ringing and ringing. Then suddenly it stopped, and Mrs Parsnip's voice came through the intercom.

'Attention everyone! This is an emergency. I repeat this is not a drill! Would everyone please take their bags and proceed immediately to the school hall. I repeat, this is an emergency. Everyone is to go to the school hall *now*!'

'What's happening?' asked someone in the back.

Mr Farthingale shook his head. 'Right, row by row, front row first. No shoving, no running, just grab your bags and walk — not run — as fast as you can to the hall. Front row.'

Chairs scraped as kids got up.

'Second row.'

The front row kids had already grabbed their bags and were heading off through the rain.

'Third row.'

Cecil stood up. 'What do you think's wrong?' whispered Shaun behind him. Cecil shrugged.

'Can't be a bushfire,' said Jason. 'Not in this weather. Maybe someone's spilt something dangerous in the chemistry lab.'

Cecil grabbed his bag and trotted through the rain. Half the school was in the hall already, the other half heading swiftly in from the outlying buildings.

Mr Farthingale pointed to the rows near the front. He carried the roll book under his arm and had grabbed his briefcase too. All around them teachers were getting everyone seated and checking names on their rolls too.

'Mervin McIntyre.'

'Here, miss.'

'Kate Linell.'

'Here, Mrs Parsnip.'

'Shaun Delaney.'

'Here, sir.'

'Jason Jones.'

'Here, sir,' said Jason.

'Cecil, I mean CJ.'

'Here, sir,' said Cecil, peering round as the chaos in the hall turned to order.

Mrs Parsnip climbed up onto the stage. She was wearing her raincoat and hat. 'Is everyone checked off?' she called.

There was a chorus of 'yeses' from the teachers.

'Then please listen carefully. There is no need to panic, but we have to move swiftly. The Budgerigar Dam has burst up river.' There were gasps all around them. Someone screamed faintly toward the back of the hall. 'Now calm down. The floodwaters will hit us in approximately half an hour . . .' continued Mrs Parsnip.

'Now, really,' as some of the younger kids began to cry, 'we will be quite safe as long as we are sensible about this.'

Cecil craned his neck to see out the hall door. The creek looked much the same, smooth and brown and only a little higher up its banks.

'Most of the town should be all right as it's on a hill, but as you know the school is on lower ground right by the creek. So the emergency services have arranged for the school buses to pick up everyone from school and take them to safety before the flood gets here. Settle

down!' she yelled, as the buzz of cries and chatter broke out across the room. 'I said there was no need to panic!'

'Now there aren't enough buses to take everyone at once so we will start with the youngest children first. Miss Appleby, could you take your class out to the bus stop please, then Miss Lee's class and Mrs Peters'.'

Mrs Parsnip paused while the littlies left the hall, then glanced at her watch. 'There is really plenty of time,' she said, a bit uncertainly now. 'All right, I want everyone to stay in their seats until the buses come back, but you can talk among yourselves.'

Cecil sat frozen in his seat as the excited talk buzzed around him. A burst dam! A wall of water rolling down the river! Had anyone else in this room ever seen a giant wave? Had any of them any idea of the power of water?

Jason nudged him. 'Better than maths, anyway.'

'Yeah. I suppose,' said Cecil, biting his lips.

'You okay?' asked Jason.

'Yeah, I'm fine.' Cecil looked at his watch. Five minutes since the littlies had left. How long would it take for the buses to take the younger kids to high ground, then come back and take them too?

Ten minutes passed and the buses still hadn't come back. Fifteen minutes ... the water would be thundering towards them.

Mrs Parsnip's mobile phone rang. She answered it, spoke briefly, then put it away.

'The buses are on their way back,' she announced. 'I'd like you to go out quietly to the bus stop, row by row, and wait for them.'

Everyone leapt from their seats and headed out the door before she'd finished talking. Some of the kids were laughing, but others looked worried, and a few of the girls were holding hands. Cecil trudged through the rain by himself, his hands in his pockets.

The rain was even harder now, thick grey stripes spearing down from the sky. It was difficult to even see the bus stop, thought Cecil, or the oval, or the creek ... Cecil gasped. He ran over to Mr Farthingale. 'Sir! Sir!'

'What is it CJ?'

Cecil pointed. 'The creek! It's rising! Look!'

Mr Farthingale peered at the creek through the rain, as though he expected to see a wall of water plunging towards them.

There was no wall of water. But the little creek had vanished. Instead the water swirled, brown and frothy, up over the banks. Every second it rose higher and higher, eating the banks and oval in great hungry gulps. Metre after metre of ground disappeared.

Mr Farthingale took one glance at the deserted road and bus stop then made a megaphone with his hands. 'Everyone back to the hall! Now!' he yelled.

'Why should we ...?' began Big Bernie.

Cecil turned on him. 'Don't you know how to obey orders!' he yelled. 'You wouldn't last five minutes on board ship!'

Big Bernie smirked. 'Your mum's pirate ship? Hey,' he said to Jason, 'did you hear? This drip thinks his mum's a pirate.'

'I bet your mum's a blue-bummed baboon,' said Jason. 'That's how come she got a big baboon for a son. Come on!'

Mr Farthingale was already at the hall. The doors were shut. Cecil glanced back. The water was still rising steadily up the hill from the oval. It was almost at the netball courts now.

What was Mr Farthingale thinking of? The hall would be flooded in a few minutes. They'd be trapped inside and drowned!

'Okay,' yelled Mr Farthingale 'I want everyone up on the hall roof. Mrs Parsnip and I will give you a leg up. I want two of the bigger boys — yes, you Shaun and Jason. Up you go first then you can reach down and help the others up. Right, Jason . . .'

Jason put his foot on Mr Farthingale's and Mrs Parsnip's hands and as they heaved, sprang up till his belly was over the eaves. He clambered the rest of the way then leant down to help Shaun.

'No way!' Big Bernie shoved his way to the front and elbowed Shaun out of the way. 'I'm going next! I'm not waiting for the flood to get me!'

He looked back nervously. The football oval was deep under water now, brown and swirling.

Mr Farthingale looked like he might protest. He caught Mrs Parsnip's eye. She shrugged. It was quicker just to heave Big Bernie up.

Big Bernie's feet disappeared over the edge of the roof. Now Jason was leaning down to grab Shaun's hand, then Shaun and Jason leant over to help Maryanne, Emma, Leanne, Jack, Troy ...

Cecil hung back. No matter how scared he was, he wasn't going to push his way to the front like Big Bernie. Let the others go first.

Four more to go ... three ... two ...

'Snap!'

Cecil looked around. The flood was only a metre away now, creeping up the hill towards the hall. As he looked the water seeped across the ground to his feet, and began to lap against the wall of the hall.

'Snap!'

What was that? Cecil gazed around frantically. It had sounded like ...

'Snap!' The crocodile chewed at a discarded hot dog and stared at him from under the rubbish bins.

'What are you doing here you dumb crocodile?' yelled Cecil.

Snap stared at him as though to say, 'aren't you glad I'm here to keep you company?'

Cecil bit his lip. Snap must have followed him to school! He must have been worried about him and swam up the creek.

'You stupid crocodile!' yelled Cecil. 'The flood will sweep you away! Come over here at once!'

'Crocodile!' squeaked Mrs Parsnip. 'Is that a crocodile? But there aren't any crocodiles in Bandicoot Creek!'

'Get back, CJ!' yelled Mr Farthingale. 'That thing looks dangerous!'

'He's not dangerous!' explained Cecil. 'He's a pet!'

'A pet crocodile!' Mrs Parsnip protested. 'But we don't allow pets at school!'

'Come here, you dopey reptile!' yelled Cecil again. Snap blinked at him, confused. 'Hurry!' screamed Cecil. The water was halfway up to his knees now.

Snap didn't move.

'CJ! Up on the roof! Now!!' shouted Mr Farthingale.

'I can't leave Snap.' cried Cecil. He began to wade over to the rubbish bin.

'Don't go near that crocodile!' shrieked Mrs Parsnip. She looked like she didn't know whether to be more scared of the flood or the crocodile.

'CJ, the water's rising fast!' shouted Mr Farthingale.

Snap thrashed his tail in the murky water. 'Snap?' he asked. He sounded worried.

'It's all right, boy,' called Cecil. The flood swirled around Cecil's knees. He could feel the water tug him now, cold and ruthless. 'Swim over to me, Snap!' he cried.

The crocodile looked down at him as though to say, 'no, you come here and we'll go back to the ship. I don't like this place!'

The water tugged at Cecil's waist.

'We'll both drown if you don't come,' shouted Cecil.

Suddenly Snap moved. One minute he was cowering in the water under the rubbish bin, the next he was swimming through the water and leaping up onto Cecil's shoulder.

'Ow!' cried Cecil, as twenty kilos of crocodile skin, tail and bad breath landed on him, then common sense took over. He began wading back towards the hall, with Snap hanging over his shoulder like a wet crocodile-skin towel.

The flood was chest high now. The current pushed and pulled at him; Cecil forced himself forwards. He'd never make it! The water was too high, the current too strong. He'd left it too long!

A strong hand grasped his. 'You'll be right!' yelled Mr Farthingale above the noise of the water, as he pulled Cecil through the floodwaters back towards the hall.

'Hurry!' shouted Mrs Parsnip, eyeing Snap doubtfully. She held Mr Farthingale's other hand in hers, steadying them both as they forced their way through the flood.

The water was too deep now for him to stand on the teachers' hands. Instead Mr Farthingale hoisted Cecil (complete with crocodile stole) up onto his shoulders. Up on the roof Shaun and Jason leant down, their hands reaching for his.

Snap grunted in his ear, his claws digging even deeper into his shoulder, his jaws reaching up to Jason and Shaun's hands ...

'Don't bite their fingers off, you dumb crocodile,' yelled Cecil. 'They're trying to help us! This is no time for a snack!'

Snap closed his jaws. Jason and Shaun each grabbed one of Cecil's hands and pulled him upwards. Up ... up ... up ... His wrists felt like they might break with the weight of his body and Snap's too. His belly grazed against the guttering.

Then suddenly he was on the roof, gasping and trying to catch his breath, while Shaun and Jason hauled up Mrs Parsnip as Mr Farthingale heaved her up from below.

'Ooof!' said Mrs Parsnip, as she landed belly down. She looked up at once. 'Everyone keep away from that crocodile!' she ordered.

'He won't hurt anyone!' gasped Cecil, as Snap gave a sharp 'Snap!' as though to say, that was a rough ride up, and crawled off his shoulder onto the roof. Someone screamed, but Cecil was too tired to take any notice.

It was Mr Farthingale's turn now. Shaun and Jason reached down towards him, while Cecil tried to get his breath.

Suddenly a hand shook his shoulder. 'CJ, we can't reach Mr Farthingale!' yelled Jason above the noise of the flood and rain. 'There's no one down there to help him get up here!'

Cecil hauled himself upright, staggered to the edge of the roof and peered down. The water was almost up to Mr Farthingale's shoulders now. 'Can't he climb up part of the way?'

Jason shook his head. 'There's nothing to hang on to!'

Cecil thought fast. When you came aboard ship, you climbed the ladder, and if there was no ladder, the crew cast down a rope. 'Quickly!' he yelled. 'Take your tracksuit pants off!'

'What?'

'You heard me! Fast!' Cecil stripped off his own tracksuit bottoms as he spoke.

Big Bernie giggled behind him then whistled.

'Nice underpants!' Then he gulped as Snap suddenly turned his grinning jaws in his direction. 'Hey, is that crocodile *real*?'

Try stuffing your fingers in his mouth and find out, jellyfish belly, thought Cecil, but he didn't bother saying it aloud. He grabbed Jason's tracksuit pants, then Shaun's, and twisted them together with his own and knotted them.

'What are you doing?' yelled Jason, above the noise of the flood.

'Making a rope! One pair of pants wouldn't be strong enough, but if I tie them together, they should take Mr Farthingale's weight.'

Cecil threw the tracksuit rope down to Mr Farthingale. Mr Farthingale grabbed it. The water was at his shoulders now, and he had to keep hold of the drainpipe to stop being swept away. But he shook his head. 'I'll pull you off the roof if I tug on this,' he called.

'No, you won't!' yelled Cecil. 'Jason, hang on to the rope on my left, and Shaun, you hang on to the right. Now everyone get behind one of us and grab hold of the person in front like a tug of war. When I say heave, *heave*!'

The class lined up behind them. Only Big Bernie hung back and finally, even he joined in so as not to be left out.

'Heave!' yelled Cecil. 'Mr Farthingale, leap!'

Mr Farthingale leapt. For a moment his legs dangled in the water, then slowly, slowly, they dragged him up, up, up . . .

'Ooof,' said Mr Farthingale, as he landed on his tummy on the roof.

'Snap?' said Snap. He crawled onto Mr Farthingale's back and settled down comfortably.

'Get off, you dumb crocodile,' gasped Cecil, shoving him off with his foot. 'That's a teacher, not a cushion!'

Suddenly his legs wouldn't hold him any more. He unknotted his pants, pulled them back on shakily and collapsed down onto the hall roof. Snap crawled over to him and put his snout in Cecil's lap.

Shaun and Jason pulled their pants on too, keeping a wary eye on Snap. 'Hey, is that crocodile, um, like *dangerous*?' asked Jason.

'No,' said Cecil. 'Well, a bit,' he added honestly. 'He does eat slavers and . . . well, bad people. He chews their fingers and toes anyway.'

'What *sort* of bad people?' asked Big Bernie, moving his feet away nervously.

Cecil shrugged. It was a little warmer with his pants on, but not much. The rain dripped and drizzled down his hair.

'What's going to happen now?' Big Bernie looked down at the raging water. He seemed to have shrunk in the last hour.

Mrs Parsnip tried to smile. 'There's really nothing to worry about,' she said, a little shakily 'I'm sure the flood won't come any higher. And if it does, well, someone is sure to rescue us!'

'How?' demanded Big Bernie. 'There isn't any boat around here big enough to take us all!'

'Yes, there is,' said Cecil.

Big Bernie rolled his eyes. 'Oh, yeah? Your mum's pirate ship I suppose?'

'Yes,' said Cecil.

'Huh,' said Big Bernie, recovering himself a little. 'Just because you've got a crocodile doesn't mean you've got a pirate ship too! Hands up who believes in CJ's pirate ship?' he looked around triumphantly.

Immediately Jason and Shaun put their hands up.

Cecil blinked. 'Hey, thanks,' he whispered.

Then slowly Mr Farthingale stood up and put his hand up too. Mrs Parsnip stared. 'You really don't think . . .' she began.

Mr Farthingale grinned. 'Listen,' he said.

Suddenly everyone on the roof was quiet. The only sounds were the mutter of the flood and the beat of the rain and the crash of logs and sticks as they swirled against the hall walls, and . . .

'With a yo ho ho and you'll walk the plank.

The deck was slimy, the galley stank,

The porridge smelt of seagull doo;

The briny deep's too good for you!'

'Here they come!' yelled Cecil, as the good ship *Mermaid* sailed across the brown and boiling water where Bandicoot Creek had once flowed peacefully before the flood. He ran to the other end of the hall roof, the tin clanging damply under his feet. 'Hey, Mum!' he yelled, as he waved his arms. 'We're over here!'

'Ahoy, shipmate!' yelled Harry the Hook from the crow's nest. 'The Captain heard on that radio thingy you bought her for

Mother's Day that you lot were having some trouble up here! Thought we'd see if we could lend a hand. Or a hook!' he added.

Mrs Parsnip sat down suddenly in a puddle on the roof. 'It ... it ... it *is* a pirate ship!' she stuttered.

Big Bernie blinked. 'Is that a *real* sword she's waving?' he breathed.

'Hey, cool,' breathed Jason. 'They're flying the skull and crossbones!'

'Look at all those sails,' cried Shaun.

'Hi, Mum,' said Cecil.

Chapter 14

Saved From the Flood

Filthy Frederick tossed the grappling hook over to the roof and the good ship *Mermaid* pulled alongside the hall.

'Right,' ordered Mum, marching up and down the deck with her hands on her hips. 'Step lively now, you varmints! Last one on board's a blubber-bellied bull ant!'

The kids of Bandicoot Flats Central School clambered over the rails and onto the good ship *Mermaid*. Cecil handed Snap to Filthy Frederick. Snap looked relieved to get back on board. He crawled over to a pile of rope, lay down and shut his eyes.

Mum strode up to Mrs Parsnip and
held out her hand. 'Captain Tania the
Terrible at your service,' she said.

'Er ... I'm Mrs Parsnip,' said Mrs Parsnip.

Mum beamed. 'Then you're the school principal,' she
cried. 'The captain of the school, that right?'

'Er, yes,' said Mrs Parsnip.

Mum nodded. 'Tell me, M'lady Principal, what do
you find is best for keeping discipline? Do you make the
kids walk the plank or do you clap them in irons in the
school dungeon and let the rats nibble their toes?'

'Er ...' said Mrs Parsnip. 'Usually detention.'

Big Bernie went pale. He nudged Cecil. 'Does your
mum *really* clap people in irons?' he whispered.

'No, of course not,' said Cecil. 'Mum is totally against
people being clapped in irons.'

Big Bernie breathed out again. 'Of course I
knew she wouldn't ...' he began.

'She just makes them walk the
plank,' said Cecil.

Big Bernie went even
paler. Cecil grinned. He
didn't think Big Bernie
needed to know that
Mum only made people
walk the plank if there
was an island nearby.

Mrs Parsnip looked a bit pale too. Mum patted her arm sympathetically. 'Why don't you go below, m'lady, and let Putrid Percival make you a nice tankard of tea?' she suggested. 'And maybe a bowl of good hot sea monster soup too.'

'Th — thank you,' stuttered Mrs Parsnip. 'Er ... not the soup. I'm sure it's delicious but ...' Suddenly she turned green and dashed for the side of the ship.

Shaun looked over the rail. 'Hey, she had a salad sandwich for lunch.'

'How do you know?' asked Jason.

'Because I just saw it float off in the flood. There were green bits and red bits and brown bits and ...'

'Ooohh,' groaned Mrs Parsnip.

'Seasick,' said Mum. 'Shark-eyed Pete, fetch the lady some of Cecil's turtle dung and vampire bat seasickness potion. Maybe you'd better get her a bucket too. Barnacle Bruce, help the lady down the companionway and put her in my bed. It's a good potion but it makes you sleep,' she added to Mr Farthingale. 'Now trim the sails, you scurvy mongrels!' she yelled to the rest of the crew. 'Let's get this ship underway!'

Mum grinned at Mr Farthingale. 'We'll have you

back on dry land before you can say, "there goes breakfast overboard".'

Jason looked eagerly at Mr Farthingale. 'Sir, do we have to go back to dry land straightaway?'

'Eh?' asked Mr Farthingale.

'Couldn't we go for a sail? Just a little one?'

'Well, I ... er ... you'd have to ask the captain,' said Mr Farthingale. 'And Mrs Parsnip.'

Mum beamed. 'It would be a pleasure,' she said.

'I'll go ask Mrs Parsnip,' offered Shaun. He disappeared down the ladder, only to reappear a minute later. 'She just said "anything! anything!" and groaned,' he reported.

'Hasn't found her sea legs yet,' said Mum. 'She'll be grand once she gets a bit of potion in her. Right, head her out to sea and through the time warp thingy, boys!'

'Time warp?' asked Mr Farthingale.

Mum nodded. 'That's how young Cecil here gets to school. The wizard showed us.' She grinned at Mr Farthingale. 'Filthy Frederick was right, you know. You are a fine figure of a man!'

Mr Farthingale blushed.

The good ship *Mermaid* changed course. Soon the land was distant, grey and shadowed. The rain had eased to a gentle drizzle but the clouds hung low. Even the seagulls were silent.

Then all at once the light changed. The air grew blue, then green, then gold. You could almost hear the sparkles in the air. Suddenly the air was clear again; the rain had gone, and the land behind had vanished too. The sun beamed down from a cloudless sky.

'Wow!' yelled Jason. He ran to the rail. 'We're out at sea!'

'And back in the past,' Cecil told him. 'No computers, no phones. Just sailing ships and sea monsters and ...'

'Slaver to starboard, Captain!' cried Harry the Hook. 'By thunder! It's the *Black Ship*! She's headed this way!'

'The *Black Ship*!' Mum ran to the rail too. 'The *Black Ship* is the biggest slave ship in all these waters!' she told Mr Farthingale. 'If only we could catch her! But she's too fast for us. As soon as she sees us she runs away.'

'What's that noise?' demanded Big Bernie.

'It's the groans of the slaves,' said Cecil 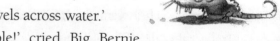 quietly. 'Sound travels across water.'

'But it's horrible!' cried Big Bernie.

'What could make people cry like that?'

'Being trapped in a dark hold with rats and bound by chains,' said Mum shortly, 'with nothing to look forward to but whips and slavery.'

Mum shaded her eyes. 'Yes, she's going about. We'll never catch her, lads.'

'But you can't just let her get away!' cried Mr Farthingale. 'We have to at least try to rescue the slaves!'

'No use,' said Mum. 'Don't think we haven't tried, time out of mind, to catch up with them. But she's bigger than the *Mermaid*, with more sail. And they can blow us out of the water while we dare not use our cannon, for fear of hitting the slaves too.'

'Wait a minute.' Suddenly Cecil had an idea. He stared at the big ship on the horizon. 'You said she was headed this way?'

'She was indeed.' Mum nodded.

'But she turned around when she saw us?'

'That's it,' said Mum.

'So if we weren't here, she might head this way again?'

'Yes. What's wrong with you, lad? Has all that reading made your brain slow?'

'No, Mum, listen!' insisted Cecil. 'Why don't we go back through the time warp! Then we can wait till you think the *Black Ship* has had time to get here, and zap out through the time warp again and grab them!'

Mum said nothing for a moment. Cecil's face fell. 'You don't think it would work?'

Mum nodded slowly. Suddenly she grinned. 'You're a genius, lad! Why, it's enough to make me take up reading too!' she cried. 'Well, almost,' she added. 'Filthy Frederick!' she yelled. 'Take us back the way we came! Hurry, you poxy varmint! Hurry!'

'Aye aye, Captain,' called Filthy Frederick.

One minute ... two minutes ... suddenly the light changed again. The rain drizzled around them as the coast appeared once more, the township smudged and grey in the distance.

'We need to wait ten minutes, I reckon,' said Mum, glancing up at where the sun would have been if the clouds hadn't covered it.

Suddenly Mr Farthingale looked worried. 'The kids!' he said. 'I ... I can't take them hunting slavers! You have to drop them off where they'll be safe!'

'But there's no time!' cried Mum. 'We'll lose her again!'

'You can't put us off, sir!' Jason and Shaun ran up to Mr Farthingale. 'We want to get the *Black Ship* too!'

'You heard the slaves!' yelled Big Bernie. His face was pale, but he didn't look as scared as he had back at the flood. 'They'll never be free if we don't rescue them!'

'Um,' said Mr Farthingale.

'Everyone who's frightened go below!' yelled Mum. 'That sit right with you, teacher? But everyone who has the stomach for a fight grab a sword!'

There was a buzz of excitement on the deck. No one went below.

'Swords!' yelled Jason. 'Cool!'

'Are you *sure* it's safe?' said Mr Farthingale doubtfully.

Mum grinned. 'No. Life isn't safe! One minute you can be safe on your ship and next minute a typhoon can sweep you into the sea, or the pox take you, or a sea monster swallow you whole. But while there's breath in us and life, let's live it! And help others live it too!'

Then Mr Farthingale grinned back. 'Hand me a sword!' he declared.

'On second thoughts,' decided Mum, 'maybe you lot of landlubbers had better have your first go with swords some other day. I don't want anyone cutting off hands and feet accidentally! Let's go with plan number two! Putrid Percival!' she yelled.

'Yes Captain!' shouted Putrid Percival from the galley.

'Bring up the buckets of old sea monsters' guts!'

'Aye aye, Captain!' cried Putrid Percival.

'Sea monsters' guts?' inquired Mr Farthingale. 'How do you fight with sea monsters' guts?'

'You'll see!' said Mum. 'Right, you young varmints. As soon as I yell "Jump!", all of you jump onto the *Black Ship* and hold onto the rail. Got it?'

'Got it!' yelled Bandicoot Flats Central School.

'Buckets of bubbling guts coming up, Captain,' puffed Putrid Percival, as he, Filthy Frederick, Barnacle Bruce and Ambrose One Arm lugged buckets of yuck

up the companionway. Muffled glups came from the buckets and the odd white maggot crawled from under the lids.

'Eweerk! They pong!' cried Shaun.

'All the better!' declared Mum. 'Haul them up! That's right, boys!' She glanced up again to where the sun should be. 'Well lads — and lasses too, of course — this is it. Everyone obey orders!'

'Aye aye, Captain,' chorused six pirates, twenty kids and a teacher.

'Right! Back through the time warp then!' yelled Mum, waving her pirate hat in the air so the rain danced on her hair.

Gold light, green light, showers of sparkles, then blue sky again, white-capped waves and . . .

'The *Black Ship* ahoy, Captain!' shouted Harry the Hook from the crow's nest.

It *was* the *Black Ship*, looming up only metres away from them. It was so close Cecil could hear the whips below as the slaves cried with despair, deep in the hold.

For a moment Cecil looked at the *Black Ship* uncertainly. It was so very big and so very black, with cannon poking out of every porthole. But there was no time now for the *Black Ship* to aim their cannon.

'Get the grappling hooks!' shouted Mum. 'Don't let her get away! Cecil, into the coil of rope!'

'No way!' shouted Cecil. 'I'm fighting too this time!'

'But you hate piracy . . .' began Mum.

'It's different now!' declared Cecil, and somehow it was. Somehow being with your friends made all the difference.

'Swing your buckets!' called Mum.

Up on the maindeck the pirates grabbed their buckets and threw their contents with all their might. An avalanche of sea monsters' guts rained down on the *Black Ship*'s decks, all green and black and bubbling putrid pink.

'What the . . . ?' The captain of the *Black Ship* looked up from the wheel and stared. 'Where did you come from? What's this muck? It stinks! Magic!' he roared, picking rotten sea monster from his beard.

'No magic, you black-hearted varmint!' shouted Mum. 'Or not much anyway,' she added. 'Take that, you rat-whiskered rogue!'

Mum leapt over the rails of the good ship *Mermaid* and onto the deck of the *Black Ship*. Cecil started to go after her. Filthy Frederick held him back. 'Not till Captain says, matey. Always obey orders.'

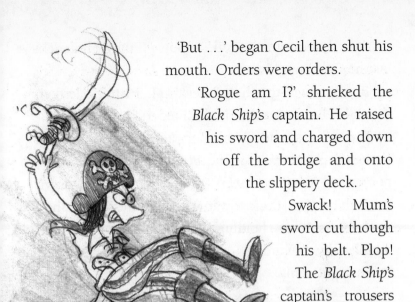

'But ...' began Cecil then shut his mouth. Orders were orders.

'Rogue am I?' shrieked the *Black Ship's* captain. He raised his sword and charged down off the bridge and onto the slippery deck.

Swack! Mum's sword cut though his belt. Plop! The *Black Ship's* captain's trousers fell down. 'Glub!' cried the *Black Ship's* captain, as he tripped over his trousers and tumbled face first into the sea monsters' guts. 'Men!' he screamed, lifting his head and spitting out a slimy orange tentacle. 'Attack!'

Up the companionway, onto the slippery deck ran the slavers.

'Arrk!' cried the first one, as he saw the last remnants of long-eaten sea monsters oozing over the deck. 'The pong! The stink!'

'Now!' bellowed Mum.

Over the rails swarmed the crew of the good ship *Mermaid*: six pirates with their swords, twenty kids and a teacher.

'Now hold onto the rail,' shouted Filthy Frederick. 'As the Captain told us to.'

'But how will that help?' began Mr Farthingale then shook his head. 'Aye aye, Filthy Frederick,' he said.

The pirates and Bandicoot Flats Central School clustered at the rails of the *Black Ship*, as the slavers poured up the *Black Ship*'s companionway and down from the upper deck towards them, dressed in their steel breastplates holding halberds and pikes and double-edged swords.

Then suddenly . . .

CHAPTER 15

The End of the Black Ship

All at once the *Black Ship* began to tilt with the weight of the kids and the pirates and the *Black Ship*'s crew, who were thundering towards them. And as the decks tilted, the slavers stepped in the slimy, slippery sea monsters' guts and . . .

'They're all sliding overboard!' yelled Jason, holding tight to the rail.

'Yep!' grinned Mum, one boot on the *Black Ship*'s captain's back. She gave him a neat kick. 'Off with you too, matey!'

'Gloop!' said the Captain, his mouth full of maggots. Mum gave him a shove and he slid down into the sea.

Cecil peered over and looked down at him. 'Don't worry!' he yelled. 'It's nice and clean in the water! It'll wash off the maggots!'

'But I can't swim!' bleated the *Black Ship's* captain, paddling and splashing furiously.

'Oh, throw him a lifebelt, someone,' said Mum, stepping down off the bridge and onto the deck. 'Frederick, Ambrose, Harry, go down and unchain the slaves and . . .'

'Mum!' shrieked Cecil. A final, unseen slaver had crept along the bridge, just above her, his sword in his hand.

Cecil thrust himself forward. 'Don't touch my mother, doggie dribble!' he roared.

Whump! Cecil grabbed the slaver's knees and brought him down onto the slimy deck.

'A perfect tackle!' yelled Mr Farthingale.

Mum grinned. 'Thanks, son. Looks like you learnt something from all that feetball.'

'Eeerk,' said Cecil, wiping sea monsters' guts off his tracksuit. It had been wet and muddy before, but now it smelt like the school garbage bins that time the meat pies went bad in the tuck shop.

Big Bernie lumbered over. 'You stink,' he offered helpfully. 'Hey, do you need a hand throwing him over the side?'

'Yeah, sure. Thanks,' said Cecil, surprised. He grabbed the slaver's feet while Big Bernie grabbed his arms.

'One, two, three!' yelled Jason, as Cecil and Big Bernie heaved the slaver overboard.

'Right, that's the last of them,' said Mum briskly. 'Now I want everyone hauling up buckets of water to clean this deck.'

'Why?' asked Jason.

'Because it's the slaves' ship now,' said Mum soberly. 'And they deserve better than mucky decks. Good Queen Bess wants her treasure — and we take a bit of that ourselves — but the real business here is freeing the slaves. With a ship to sail home in and a share of the treasure, they'll be safe and free.'

CHAPTER 16

Freedom

One by one the slaves ventured out on deck, blinking in the sunlight: kids with big eyes, women with scared, silent faces, men who had been whipped and chained.

'Snail-gutted slavers,' muttered Mum watching the slaves from the deck of the good ship *Mermaid* and wiping away a few tears with the big hanky with the skull and crossbones embroidered on the corner that Cecil had given her for a Mother's Day present. 'Well, at least they're free now.'

'Ahoy, Captain!' Filthy Frederick hailed her from the *Black Ship*. 'A couple of the men here are shanghaied sailors. One says he's a master navigator. Reckon this lot will be safe on their own.'

'Good speed to them!' called Mum. 'Now bring over our share of the treasure!'

She turned to the kids. 'Half the treasure for the slaves, a quarter for Good Queen Bess and a quarter for us.'

'Only a quarter!' protested Jason. 'That's not very much.'

'You wait till you see the treasure,' said Mum.

One by one the pirates carried the treasure on board.

'Eight chests of jewels,' said Cecil, making a note on his list, 'two hundred and forty gold bars — no, Snap, you can't eat gold bars, you'll break a tooth — one hundred and sixty bolts of chinese silk, sixteen chests of pepper — pepper is worth more than gold in London,' he told Jason and Shaun who were standing nearby. 'Eighty-eight barrels of cinnamon bark — that's worth even more than pepper. Snap, I told you pepper makes you sneeze if you sniff too closely.'

'Atchoo!' sneezed Snap again.

Mr Farthingale blinked. 'You must be millionaires,' he whispered.

Mum shrugged. 'Who counts? We've got a good ship and a good life and good friends; who cares how many chests of gold are back home in the attic?'

'The queen gave Cecil's dad a baronetry, too,' added Filthy Frederick proudly, picking a few fleas out of his beard and crunching them absent-mindedly between his three front teeth.

'Then you're,' Shaun worked it out, '. . . Lady Tania.'

'Just call me Captain,' said Mum, opening one of the treasure chests.

'And you're Sir Cecil!' exclaimed Jason to Cecil.

'Well, yeah,' said Cecil, embarrassed. 'But I'd rather be called CJ.'

'Go and check on M'lady Principal, Frederick,' Mum ordered. 'She should sleep for another two hours or so, but we better make sure she's all right. Now, let's have a look at this treasure.' Mum hauled ropes of pearls and diamonds out of the chest. 'Must be some here suitable for youngsters,' she muttered. 'Ah, here we are. Choose what you want from these. And here, M'lord Teacher, this is for the school.' She tossed him a bar of gold.

'Oof.' Mr Farthingale nearly dropped it. 'It's heavy!'

'Gold *is* heavy,' said Mum. 'Use it to buy more feetballs or books or something. And this is for you.' She tossed him a sword. The jewels in its hilt flashed in the sunlight. 'And any time you want a lesson in how to use it . . .' Mum winked, 'just give me a hoy.'

The kids crowded around. There were piles of rings, their giant diamonds glowing even in the shade of the sails, gold cat brooches with emerald eyes and daggers with sapphires on their hilts . . .

('No daggers,' said Mr Farthingale firmly, peering over their heads.

'But, sir, they're just fruit knives,' said Jason innocently, 'to peel oranges and things.')

. . . ruby buttons, gold cups with yellow diamonds around their rims, golden balls . . .

('They're not much use,' said Shaun. 'They don't even bounce. Hey, there isn't a golden computer game in there, is there?')

...small boxes made of pearls and silver that played strange songs when they were opened, jewelled birds that sang when you pressed their golden tails, and a big wide vase-like thing, that was copper outside and gold inside.

'What's that thing?' demanded Jason.

'It's a chamber pot,' explained Cecil, 'for, er, you know, when you don't have an ensuite bathroom and can't reach the porthole. It goes under the bed.'

He hesitated. 'Anyone mind if I take that one?' he asked. 'Snap can eat his dinner out of it.'

'One of each for everyone,' said Mum briskly.

Big Bernie looked up
from the treasure.
'The slaves get stuff
like this too?'
'Yes,' said
Mum gently.
'So they're rich?'
Mum nodded.
'They deserve to be,
after all they've gone through,' she said.

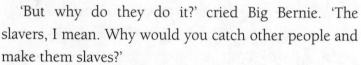

'But why do they do it?' cried Big Bernie. 'The
slavers, I mean. Why would you catch other people and
make them slaves?'

'Because they can,' said Mum simply. 'Some people
think that if you're strong enough to do something, why
then, you can just go ahead and do it. They don't
wonder if it's right. They just don't think at all.'

She blew her nose, sniffed twice, then put away her
hanky. 'To my way of thinking you should use what
you've got to make the world better, not worse. Boats or
muscles, lad, you use what you have.'

Filthy Frederick's wooden leg clattered across the deck.
'Mrs Parsnip's fast asleep, Captain,' he reported. 'I looked
in on her and she opened her eyes and said, "When did
you last have a bath?" then went back to sleep again.'

'When *did* you last have a bath Filthy Frederick?'
asked Cecil curiously.

Filthy Frederick scratched his head, dislodging three fleas, a kilo of dandruff and a bit of old sea monster tentacle. 'Ten years ago, was it? No, make that twenty. It was the year we captured that Egyptian queen. She had a gold bath, all filled with goat's milk. Ah, I was younger in those days ...'

Mum sniffed again. 'Speaking of baths, me hearties, we stink of sea monsters' guts! How about we find us a desert island with a good sandy beach and wash the pong off? Then maybe we can catch us another sea monster. There's nothing better than fresh sea monster grilled on a driftwood fire with a few coconuts. Then we can ...'

'Ahem,' coughed Mr Farthingale. 'I think I really should be getting the kids back.'

'Don't worry about that!' boomed Mum, slapping him on the back. 'Remember the time warp thingy!'

'Yes, but ...' began Mr Farthingale.

'How do you think we get Cecil to school on time every day? We just think of what time we want it to be when we go through the time warp, and it is.'

'So ...' Mr Farthingale worked it out. 'We can stay here in the past as long as we like and still get back before anyone starts to worry?'

'Exactly,' said Mum.

And so they did.

Chapter 17

Off to the Next Adventure

Up in the prow Shark-eyed Pete was showing a mob of kids how to navigate, and in the stern Filthy Frederick was teaching the others his favourite songs.

'Yo ho ho it's the life for us,

As grand as a pimple all full of pus.

A pirate ship's more fun than a bus!

It's a pirate's life for us.'

Cecil leant on the railing with the wind in his face. Someone coughed behind him.

'Ahem, er, um, CJ ...' It was Mr Farthingale. 'Ahem ... CJ ... I was wondering. Would you mind if I took your mum to the movies some night? If she wants to, of course.'

'Fine by me,' said Cecil. He thought for a minute. 'Why don't you get her to show you how to steer the ship? She's up on the bridge now.'

'I wouldn't be disturbing her?'

'Nope,' said Cecil. He didn't mind at all. Mum was lonely sometimes, even with all her crew, and Mr Farthingale was okay.

Mr Farthingale wandered off.

'With a yo ho ho and we'll sail away,

With jewels and gold and doubloons for pay,

Across the vast blue briny sea.

It's a pirate's life for me!'

sang Filthy Frederick, and some of the kids had joined in.

It was good to be on board ship again, thought Cecil. School was good too and it was going to be even better now, but he did miss the wind in his face.

Footsteps sounded across the deck — feet in joggers, not the bare feet of the pirates or Filthy Frederick's wooden leg. Big Bernie leant on the rail beside Cecil, with Shaun and Jason on his other side. They gazed out at the sea for a minute.

'Hey, look, dolphins!' cried Jason suddenly.

'They're playing in the wake of the ship,' said Cecil. 'You know, the wake is the waves we make behind us. We often see dolphins.'

'And whales?' asked Shaun.

Cecil nodded. 'Ambrose One Arm says he saw a mermaid once, too.'

They watched the dolphins grinning as they dived and leapt in the spray.

'So your Mum really is a pirate,' said Big Bernie wonderingly.

'Yes,' said Cecil. 'Well, a privateer anyway.'

'Um, I'm sorry ...' began Big Bernie.

Cecil waved him silent. 'Forget about it,' he said.

'Hey,' said Jason. 'How do you catch a sea monster?'

'You need the right bait,' explained Cecil. 'First of all you get a really big net, then you ...'

The seagulls yelled overhead, the wind smelt of sun and salt and, sitting on the wrinkle between the sea and sky, a small island shimmered in its ring of surf and sand.

The wind filled the white sails of the good ship *Mermaid* and carried her like a bird across the waves.

EPILOGUE

Wednesday is sports' afternoon at Bandicoot Flats Central School. The kids can choose which sport they want to play. There's netball on the netball courts. There's feetball on the oval.

Or on the good ship *Mermaid* you can fish for sea monsters or practise swordsmanship. You can study twenty ways to cook a sea monster with Putrid Percival, or the care and feeding of crocodiles with Snap, or learn how geometry can help you to navigate by the stars with Mr Farthingale.

And if a slave ship comes sailing by, you can practise a bit of piracy too; though, as Cecil's mum keeps pointing out, it's not *really* piracy when you have permission from the queen.

Every Wednesday afternoon the good ship *Mermaid* is packed with kids, and on the good ship *Mermaid*, Wednesday afternoon lasts as long as you like.

Everyone agrees that Bandicoot Flats Central School has the best sports' afternoon of any school around. Which makes sense of course, because Bandicoot Flats

Central is the best school in the world! As Filthy
Frederick says:

'With a yo ho ho and a school at sea,
With lots of adventures in piracy,
We'll capture ships and set slaves free,
We'll bury our treasure all tidily,
And still be home in time for tea.
It's a pirate's life for me!'

JE
Fre
c. 1

JUN   2004

3 6497 011903115

DATE DUE	
ING AUG 2 0 2004	
ING NOV 1 0 2004	
ING AUG 1 1 2005	
'NG SEP - 5 2006	